# Th

# Mysterious

# Mansion

## A Ghost Story

## Hank Roberts

## Philip L. Levin

*Philip L. Levin*
*7/01/2020*

Publishing Page

Published by Doctor's Dreams Publishing
PO Box 4808
Biloxi, MS 39535, USA
writerpllevin@gmail.com

Prepared and published in the United States of America


ICBN:


Acknowledgments: This book is a combination of efforts. Hank
Roberts had the original ideas and created an original

manuscript. This version has extensive editing and rewriting with creative input by Dr. Levin.

Chapter 1

Marley Robbins felt the summer Alabama sun baking him like an Alabama pig roast. Scratchy in his Salvation Army bought suit, he had walked three blocks over steaming concrete from the Greenwell train station. Now he stood outside the brick windowless building with the sign, "Station 47," hanging above the door. Staring at his watch, he waited until the second hand reached the top, so that at exactly two o'clock he rang the studio's doorbell.

A minute passed.

He turned to look at a woman walking by pushing a stroller. He gave her a smile and a wave and was pleased when she returned them both. Small town friendliness, he decided.

He was about to press the bell again when the door opened to reveal a mid-height balding man wearing an open collared shirt with food stains.

Marley held out his hand. "Uh. Mr. Chester Cohen?"

The fat man engulfed Marley's hand with his own, shaking it vigorously. "Yep, yep. You bet! You must be Marvin Roberts."

"Uh, Marley Robbins. You, uh, told me to be here at two, right?"

Chester checked his watch. "Punctual, huh? I like that in an employee. Yep, yep. Sure do. Well, come on in, young fellow. Follow me to my little office and we can talk."

Marley stepped in, surveying the filming studio they passed through. It had three cameras set up facing a green screen background, with a couple of chairs and other props scattered around the floor space. They entered Chester's office, a space mostly filled by a small desk and a couple of plastic chairs. On top of a file cabinet a black tabby stared down at Marley.

Chester settled in the chair behind his desk. "Have a seat, have a seat."

Marley saw that both chairs overflowed with stacks of paper, so he remained standing.

Chester reached up and scratched the sweat spot under his left armpit. "Glad you could come be a part of Station 47, Mr. Roberts. I loved your resumé. Checked out all your YouTube videos, too. Say, you want to know what made me decide to hire you?"

Marley, who had been studying the way Chester picked his nose while he talked, realized he hadn't been paying attention. He reran what he had heard the man say and replied, "Yes, sir. What made you hire me?"

"Your YouTube video about that cat farm." Chester pointed at his cat. "I liked your style – homey – local. I think a report like that every now and then will really catch on here in Greenwell."

"Thank you, Mr. Cohen. I hope I'll please you. By the way, how's your gout?"

"Gout?" Mr. Cohen cocked one eyebrow. "How did you know I have gout?"

Marley nodded at Chester's hand. "It shows in the knuckles, you know. Also," he pointed to under one of the chairs, "I saw the slippers with one toe cut out."

Mr. Cohen chortled. "Ha! You're a bright one, aren't you? You can call me Chester. Come along, fellow. I'll introduce you to your co-worker. She's the one that makes the studio work, so you better get along with her."

The walked out of the manager's office, back through the studio, and into the production chamber, a darkened room with three computer monitors running. On the wall four muted television screens showed various channels.

"Allie Burton, I'd like you to meet Marty Roberts. He's the newscaster I just hired."

Marley watched her peek up from around her computer screen. Limp brown hair framed her freckled cheeks. She wore no makeup, and the computer screen glow made her face seem pale, even ghostly. He immediately fell in love with that face.

He held out his hand. "I'm Marley Robbins. Is it Allie?"

She pushed back her chair and took his hand with her own limp grip. "Yes, Allison Burton. Everyone calls me Allie. I do the production here at Station 47. I ... uh, I ...I'm sorry."

Marley watched Allie's face flush and she abruptly sat down, hiding behind the computer screen.

Marley stepped back. "Sorry about what?"

Mr. Cohen's large pot belly shook with his chuckle. "Allie's a bit shy, but she's good at her job. Been with me the whole six months I've owned and run this station."

"Well that's my ambition," Marley replied. "I'm going to be good at my job too." He leaned over the screen so he could see Allie, who looked up hesitantly at his attempt at a reassuring smile. "I'm sure we'll get along just fine," he insisted.

Mr. Cohen told Marley that the station didn't make a lot of money, so he'd only be paying him for three hours a day, Monday through Friday. His first responsibility would be to prepare weather reports each morning. Allie would film him and then broadcast them throughout the day, in between the old movies and sit coms that made up the station's general venue.

"After you get your feet wet, I'd like you to start doing some local features, like that cat thingy you did. Maybe we can work up to a full half hour slot in the evenings. You'll be responsible for obtaining material for your show, and you'll have to run it by me first. Okay. Any questions?"

Marley shook his head.

"Good, good. I'll see you first thing tomorrow morning. Allie, why don't you take Marvin next door to Mabel's and give him some insight into our town?"

Mr. Cohen lumbered back into his office, and Marley stood looking down on the seated production woman. "Well? Coffee at Mabel's?"

Allie shook her head without looking up.

"Oh, come on. I just stepped off the Greyhound an hour ago. If I'm going to be a reporter for Greenwell, Alabama, I need you to give me some ins and outs about life in this dusty old berg."

Again, she shook her head no.

He reached past her and picked up a book from her desk. He read the title out loud, "*The Rise and Fall of the Confederacy* by Jefferson Davis. Really? I loved this one. You can't beat a firsthand report for authenticity, even if it is a one-sided view."

Allie lifted her eyes to stare at him, perhaps the first prolonged eye contact she'd had with any man other than her father in several years. "You … you like history?"

"Oh yeah. Journalism was my major at Mississippi State, but I minored in history. I have a special yen for Civil War History."

She looked down at the book again, shuffling her feet. After a moment she looked back into his eyes. "Okay, then. Let's go get some coffee."

Mabel's Diner had that old-fashioned look, red and white checkered tiles and silver rimmed barstools. Allie led them to the furthest back booth where they settled on either side of the table. Marley gave the place his usual concentrated scan.

"Used to sell milkshakes and cigarettes, huh? I wonder what happened to the local paper?"

Allie threw him a questioning glance. "Sounds like you've done your Greenwell research."

"Not much. I just noticed the blenders gathering dust on a top shelf, so figured they used to be an item here, but not for several months at least. And there's an old advertisement for Chesterfield embossed on the window."

"That's right on," Allie said. "And how did you know the newspaper went out of business six years ago?"

Marley pointed to a series of small frames on the far wall. "There are awards for best restaurant in town and other local write-ups over there, but the last one is from several years ago, judging by the yellowing of the paper."

Mabel strolled up, a plaid apron across her generous belly and a steaming coffee pot in her right hand. Receiving nods from both Allie and Marley, she turned the two cups upright on the table and filled them. She glanced at Allie and gave Marley more than a once-over.

"You new in town?" she asked.

He stood and offered her a hand, then embarrassedly dropped it seeing as how she couldn't take it due to holding the coffee pot. "Uh, yes ma'am. My name's Marley Robbins. I've just gotten the position as head newscaster at Station 47 next door. I'm going to be an investigative reporter."

Mabel put her head back and let loose a roar of laughter. "Oh, that's rich, that's rich. 'Head newscaster' at that rinky-dink two-bit station, huh? Quite a big title. And 'investigative reporter?' This I gotta see." She laughed again. "What're you gonna investigate? Lost cats?"

Indicating his dining companion with a toss of her head, "I was wondering what kind of fellow Allie would bring into my diner. A fellow dweeb. That's great." She put the coffee pot down on the table in order to wipe the tears from her eyes. After a minute of composing herself she asked, "You two want anything besides coffee? I got some fresh peach pie."

Allie nodded vigorously. She informed Marley that Mabel's pie was renowned throughout the state, and then told Mable to bring them each a slice à la mode. The waitress left still chuckling.

Marley reached up and scratched behind his ear, muffing up the hair there so his silhouette now looked uneven, flat hair behind his left ear, exploded behind the right. "So. Greenwell, huh? What's it like?"

Allie thought through that question. "What have you heard?"

"Just what I could find on the Internet. Population 12,000 or so. Town itself is named after the Greenwell family, specifically Thomas Greenwell who founded it about 1840 to service his big cotton plantation. After the War Between the States, his son Daniel was a big benefactor of the town. I think there's a statue to him somewhere."

"Yes, right in front of town hall."

"Oh yeah, I saw that on my walk over. Didn't have time to read the inscription. Saw the War memorials around the courthouse too. Lots of history here I imagine."

He noticed Allie staring at him.

"What?"

"You said at the office you were going to be good at your job," she said. "And I was impressed with what you saw in this place. Would you mind if I gave you a little test?"

He carefully set his cup down in the middle of the saucer. "Test? What kind of test?"

She closed her eyes tightly and put her hands under the table.

"Marley, what color are my eyes?"

"They're brown with a touch of green."

She opened them up. "That's correct. And what jewelry am I wearing?"

He didn't hesitate. "You have a woven bracelet on your right wrist, one of those plastic MIA things on your left, and your right index finger holds a gold band with blue stones. In addition, of course, you have those gold loop earrings."

She nodded, bringing her hands back above the table to show him he had been exactly right. "You really do notice everything, don't you?"

"Well, maybe not everything – certainly about you, though."

She blushed and turned her face down.

"No. I didn't mean it that way." He ruffled the hairlock again. "I meant, that's what I do, you know. People I meet, I've trained myself to observe the details. Like Mabel. Did you notice she has a hearing aid in her left ear, and she's had breast cancer?"

Allie looked over at Mabel, who was coming towards them with two slices of pie, each topped with a scoop of ice cream melting into a tempting white pool in its plate. Staring, she tried to see if she could tell anything about the woman's chest.

Mable looked down at her blouse. "What, did I spill something?"

Allie shook her head. "No, no. I'm sorry. I was thinking of something else."

The waitress placed the pies down and returned to her counter.

"What did you see?" Marley asked Allie.

"Nothing. What did YOU see?"

"The left breast rides higher and seems a bit fuller. Either she had an implant or wears padding after having her breast removed."

"Couldn't she just have different size breasts?"

Marley shook his head. "Much less likely."

"A regular Sherlock Holmes, aren't you?" she said, with a strongly Southern drawled English accent.

Marley laughed. "Yes, I suppose so."

They worked on their pies in silence for a few minutes.

"Have you always wanted to be an investigative reporter?" Allie asked.

"Yeah, that's always been my dream." He gobbled down his pie and dribbled the ice cream puddle from the plate into his spoon, licking it clean. "Since I graduated from college last year, I've applied to fifty television

16

stations across the country. This was the only offer I got. So … I guess I gotta make this one work. You know of any great town mysteries I can investigate?"

Allie put her fork down, interlocking her hands on the tabletop. "Now that you mention it, there is one great big one. You mentioned Thomas and Daniel Greenwell. Well, the original Greenwell mansion still exists. It's about a half-mile off the town square on its own separate hill."

Marley shrugged. "An old mansion, huh? Period pieces I suppose. What, they give tours?"

"Nope. No one's been inside it for forty years since the last Greenwell died there."

"Yeah? Must be pretty dusty by now. So, what's the big mystery?"

She leaned forward to within a foot of his nose. In a barely audible whisper, she said, "It's haunted!"

# Chapter 2

The next morning Marley showed up at ten, dressed in his suit jacket, white collared shirt, and narrow red tie. Allie took one look at him and a huge grin erupted across her face.

"Is that what you were planning on wearing on TV?"

Marley looked down at his outfit. "Uh. Yes, why?"

"Because this is Greenwell, Alabama, that's why. You gotta look the part. Come on. We'll get you some clothes at the Goodwill store down the block."

She led him out, and at the store bought him jeans, a T-shirt with "Mabel's Diner" emblazoned across the front, and a cap featuring Greenwell's city seal prominently displayed.

Back in the studio, she showed him how to retrieve the weather report from the Internet and he wrote up copy for her to put on the teleprompter. What with equipment issues and rehearsals, it took them until one o'clock to get two weather reports filmed. Afterwards they walked next door to Mabel's for her Tuesday meatloaf and a rerun of coffee and peach pie.

"I'm super excited about your idea of my doing an investigative report on the Greenwell Mansion," Marley said. "You gonna help me?"

She gave him a shy smile. "I think I could be talked into it. I do have a minor in archeology you know."

Together they sketched out in his notebook the places they'd research for information about the family and the mansion. He said he'd go through all the local, county, and state records. She chose to research the local newspaper archives and the library.

Over the next two weeks, this is the story they put together.

# Chapter 3

Thomas Greenwell came to this part of Alabama from Virginia in 1832. Although his age was uncertain, he probably was in his early twenties at the time. He'd brought his wife with him, a woman named Sarah. Within a month of his arrival, he'd bought 1,000 acres and by 1835 had built the family mansion. Within a few years he'd purchased another 10,000 acres, creating a huge plantation where the main cash crop was cotton.

In order for the family to produce and take to market such a large volume of cotton, Thomas Greenwell depended on a massive workforce of slaves. Traveling to New Orleans every other month, Mr. Thomas, as he was known, bought anywhere between eight and fifteen slaves each trip. The sources suggested he treated them harshly, but details on that were few. On the way back he'd sell about half of what he'd purchased to local farmers, making up for all the expenses of his trip.

He was a shrewd businessman. His cotton business thrived in the pre-Civil War days, as well as several side businesses, such as brick making and raising trophy horses. The plantation consisted of slave houses, stables, and specialty shops, including a blacksmith and coopery. He even had a special building where he would take a favorite female slave of the month, a place that earned the nickname, "Uncle Tom's Cabin."

Thomas Greenwell amassed a large fortune. With their great wealth and plentiful slave labor, the Greenwell mansion became renowned for hosting festive parties. There, the other area white planters would gather for cocktails on the veranda, discuss politics, and discuss the future of cotton and the nation.

The War Between the States changed all of the South, including the Greenwells. Thomas Greenwell enlisted immediately, rising to the rank of Colonel during the war, and dying in battle at the siege of Vicksburg. Thomas' two sons chose different sides, Daniel, eighteen-years-old, joined the Confederacy while his year-younger brother, Bobby, went north. Bobby was highly decorated, though Daniel not so much, around whom rumors swirled that he'd returned home with a fortune.

After the war, the two brothers tried to continue making the plantation work, despite the labor issues caused by the emancipation of their slaves. The townsfolk wrote about the angry arguments the brothers had, often in public such as at church or in a town store. No longer were there parties at the mansion.

One weekend, Daniel ordered all the servants to stay away from the house for the next three days. When they returned, there was no sign of Bobby. Daniel claimed his brother had taken his Union uniform and his sword and rode off. No one heard a word from him ever again.

Daniel sold about half of his land and helped promote the town. The soil was fertile, and with a few small industries set up on the river, including a cotton mill and a machinery shop, the town thrived. Daniel donated funds to further the town's prosperity, including building the town hall and library.

Daniel never married. Records showed that in 1890 at the age of 47 he adopted a newborn baby named Nathan. No birth certificate existed, but a legal adoption notice rested in the old courthouse records.

Nathan's history seemed the most complex. Sent to Europe as an infant, he was raised by private nannies, and attended a series of small private schools. He studied at the Sorbonne, earning a degree in liberal arts. From there, it appeared he traveled around Europe studying the occult.

After his father's death in 1930, Nathan returned to the plantation, though he was never actually seen to arrive. Once he entered the old mansion, he never set foot out of it again. Strangely enough, no pictures of him could be found.

Once settled in, Nathan had a tall brick fence built around the mansion and a small piece of the yard surrounding it. He kept the twenty acres of the forest on the hill where his home stood and sold off all the remaining land. Through the next thirty years, his only contact with any human was an African American man who served as manservant. After the servant died in the 1950s, Nathan spent the rest of his life in isolation. He had his food and needed supplies delivered to his home's porch, with his trust fund at the bank paying all charges. Occasional strange packages came with foreign stamps, adding to the mysteries of Nathan's reclusiveness.

A newspaper obituary of only a few lines mentioned Nathan Greenwell's death in 1975, the police having to break open the back door to gain entry. They found him dead in an oversize armchair in his bedroom, death from old age.

For the next few years after Nathan's death, the mansion grounds outside the wall became a hangout for teenagers or secret lovers. Sometimes these night visitors reported seeing a candle flickering in an upstairs window. They'd report seeing someone's shadow on the shade, crossing the room or sitting in a rocking chair. At times strange noises filtered out: howls, moans, and piteous cries. In the winter, smoke billowed from the tall chimney, although no one had been in the house to light a fire. After enough of these occurrences, almost no one dared to get anywhere near the place, especially at night.

# Chapter 4

"So, what do you think?" Marley asked, after they reviewed the history they'd gathered. "Should we go investigate the Greenwell Mansion this weekend?"

Allie froze, her cup halfway to her mouth. "You mean ... actually go IN there?"

"Yes. That's exactly what I mean. Don't tell me you believe all those ghost tales I've been reporting on the evening news."

"Oh, of course not." Allie tried to smile, but couldn't get her lips to turn up. "Well, maybe a little."

Marley watched her hand tremble so much she began spilling coffee over the rim and onto Mabel's paper placemat. She set her cup down in the small brown puddle she'd made.

"Really?" he asked, his eyebrows raised.

"Yes! I'm scared to death of ghosts. While I'd absolutely love to go explore the history and artifacts there, I'm not going inside that old mansion as long as it's haunted. If you want to go, I'll drive you up and wait outside. You'll want to do it during full sunlight of course."

He reached and ruffed up that hairlock again. "No, I don't think so. This adventure definitely calls for a night visit. I'll bring a sleeping bag, a bit of food and water, and some supplies. I'm eager to see just what this ghost has to say."

Allie shook her head, and then reached up and stroked his cheek, the first time she'd touched him since that first handshake. "You must be the bravest man I've ever met."

Saturday afternoon, Allie drove Marley to the foot of the Greenwell mansion. Besides energy bars and colas, he'd brought a flashlight, bug spray, notepad, Swiss-pocketknife, and a sleeping bag. He told Allie he would prove there wasn't any ghost, just a creaky old mansion.

"Okay," she called after him. "Be sure and take plenty of photos and call me if you see a ghost."

The lock and chains securing the heavy iron gate had rusted from the weather and crumbled at Marley's touch. He pushed and the gate swung open with an eerie squeal. Inside, the grounds were a jungle of weeds growing to about six feet, just low enough so that when he stepped into the courtyard, he could see over them to get his first look at the house. He jumped when the gate slammed closed behind him.

The home, a two-story large-winged mansion, had the classic look of trim red bricks, white shutters, and a huge chimney coming out the center of the house. Vines encircled much of the building, though an upstairs window remained completely unobscured.

Beneath the thick vines and overgrowth, Marley could make out the outline of a walkway meandering through the courtyard towards the large front veranda. As he made his way along the path, he passed by several structures that he realized once had been beautiful fountains and planters. He imagined how elegant the mansion must have once been.

When he reached the front door, he reached up and used the ornate clapper to produce a loud, distinctive knock. The door creaked wide open, and for a moment Marley thought he saw a butler standing there, though the image dissipated in the blink of his eyes.

Marley cringed as a cloud of foul-smelling mildew struck his nose. He took two steps in, each one raising a cloud of dust, and stood, waiting for his eyes to fully adjust to the darkness. Pointing his flashlight, he found large pieces of furniture loomed like a foreboding forest: a tall mahogany chest, large end tables with antique lamps, and overstuffed armchairs. Spider webs and rodent droppings gave evidence to the identities of the current residents. He set his pack and bag on a table.

He walked over to the drapes, most of them moth and rat eaten, and with a swish opened them enough to let in some of the fading sunlight. Turning, his gaze fell onto two large oil paintings on the far wall. The first portrayed Thomas in all his grim glory, his black vested suit topped with a starched white shirt. In the second, Daniel, in a frock coat with vest, stood before a portrayal of his statue in the town square.

Despite its current condition, there was still the appearance of this once being a home of great wealth and importance. Massive crystal chandeliers hung from sixteen-foot high ceilings. A beautifully carved wooden border ran along the walls' upper edges and he could make out remnants of lovely murals on the ceiling. Portraits of massive landscapes depicting scenery that had once been the majestic Greenwell plantation covered much of the fine wood paneling. There were fields of cotton with slaves. There were pictures of men hunting quail and pheasant. There were forest scenes laced with large deer. Paintings of prize horses hung on both sides of the fireplace.

Marley's attention riveted on that fireplace, a massive structure at least twelve by five feet in opening and a good five or six feet deep. The mantle was constructed of the finest marble with the inside lined with bricks that each had the initials T.G embedded in them. There was a large iron grate within the concavity used to hold the logs to be burned. The size of the fireplace allowed for Marley to climb completely into its bowels. He noticed that a couple of the bricks in the back were loose. Taking these out, he discovered a small chamber hidden behind the hearth. Using his pocketknife to loosen the old plaster, he soon had made an opening large enough to squeeze inside.

The room stood about eight-foot square, with a ceiling so low Marley had to stoop to prevent bumping his head. His flashlight revealed the one item in the room, a six-foot long stone sarcophagus.

Thinking for a moment of curses he'd heard about old sarcophaguses, Marley's hands trembled as he moved the coffin's lid enough to train his light inside. It reflected back a sword handle resting on top of a white muslin cloth. Using his pocketknife to slash a six-inch hole, the drape parted to reveal beneath it a smiling skull.

# Chapter 5

After taking photos, Marley closed the sarcophagus, squeezed out of the tomb, and replaced the bricks. Crawling out of the fireplace, he proceeded to explore the other rooms on the first floor. One small closet held an old toilet, the type with the reservoir box six feet above it.

Down a short hallway he entered the dining room, a space long enough to easily hold its huge mahogany table surrounded by two-dozen chairs. Along the wall, glass-doored cabinets showed rows and rows of serving ware. There were fine crystal glasses and coffee cups with gold rims. China dishes were neatly stacked and ready to serve some 25 people. In the drawers under the counter, Marley found sterling silver cutlery and serving utensils, along with at least 100 special serving pieces. All the silver was carefully stored in large wooden boxes lined with felt. Marley imagined the dinners served here, the guests in their nineteenth century antebellum finery, laughing and bragging of how the South would win the war.

Marley stepped over the broken door leading into the kitchen, finding the large room stocked with pieces from the 1920s: an old icebox, a tin barrel sink, and a wood-burning stove. The light fixture was electric, a bare-bulb socket with frayed wiring running across the ceiling and down the wall to an old push-button switch. He opened the grate covering the stove's belly and peaked inside, finding it empty.

Along an upper wall, shiny copper pots and pans hung on hooks, neatly arranged like soldiers ready for battle. Another wall held an array of knives, including cleavers, graters, santokus – all types and shapes to cut and chop with. There was one knife missing. Strangely, unlike everything else in the house, the pots and knives weren't covered in webs or dust. In fact, they seemed to gleam in the light coming through the window.

From the kitchen there was a backdoor which he unlatched and stepped through. Here he found a water pump with a large rusted galvanized trough, big enough to wash dishes or perhaps provide water for animals. A small stone walkway led through the weeds towards the back stone wall and he imagined that, a hundred and seventy years ago, meandered down to the slave quarters.

Returning to the living room, he inspected the antique stairway leading to the upper story. It had beautiful ornate banisters with steps covered with a dingy carpeting, full of dust and rat droppings. Marley noticed that there was no dust on the handrails. He stooped down to get a close look at the stairs and thought that he could make out a faint set of footprints going up. There were none coming down.

Ascending the steps, he stopped to study the collection of very old photographs and oil paintings of members of the Greenwell family along the walls, all mounted in ornate golden frames. About halfway up the staircase hung a Daguerrean photo of a middle-aged Thomas Greenwell, a woman who Marley presumed was Sarah Greenwell, and their two sons, looking to be young teenagers. Knowing their ages, Marley figured this had to be taken just before the Civil War, so between 1855 and 1858. He studied the faces, clothing, and stances, trying to figure out their personalities from their portraits. Daniel, on the far left, seemed separate, a bit aloof. Next came Thomas standing erect, a half smile on his face. Beside him, Sarah looked down upon her youngest son, as if casting a blessing upon him. Bobby, in his turn, held his mother's hand while he looked off to the left, as if something had caught his attention, or maybe in a daydream.

At the top of the stairs, Marley found a long hallway lined on both sides with doors. Behind the first door he found a large sitting room, complete with ashtrays and decayed cigars. A chess set with pieces neatly aligned sat in one corner, bookshelves full of mouse-eaten tomes made up two of the walls, and on either side of the single window hung oil paintings of Paris.

The next door opened into a bedroom with furnishings typical of the early nineteenth century, including a large double bed, armoire, chest of drawers, and two linen-covered dressing tables. On the first, etched crystal containers with sterling silver lids held jewelry, dried powder, and combs. The second had masculine works, hairbrushes and shaving equipment neatly aligned around a mirror. In the armoire he found a dozen women's dresses and a couple of suits, including the one Thomas wore in the downstairs painting. He closed the door of what he labeled Thomas and Sarah's room, and stepped across the hall to open the next door.

This one, another bedroom, had a single-sized bed and dresser. In the bottom drawer he found a neatly folded Confederate Civil War uniform. "Daniel Greenwell's room," he muttered.

Next came a small office, hardly big enough for its magnificent rolltop desk and chair. Marley jimmied the lock with his pocketknife and rolled up the top. There he found a stack of yellow papers and a handful of old photographs. Hidden in the back of one drawer, Marley discovered a bag of coins in an old leather bag and a cedar box containing a few parchment papers with seals and stamps. He stuck the bag in his pocket and set the box on the floor of the hallway outside the door to take with him when he returned downstairs.

The next door opened into a more modernized bedroom, furnishing more typical of the 1950s, including a radio and a big box television. This and the office had been wired for electricity, and, unlike the other bedrooms, a closet had been constructed in one corner, its door secured with a strong lock. Here, beside the bed and dresser, sat a large overstuffed chair. Marley realized that this chair matched the description the police reported as where Nathan had been found dead. A tremble went through Marley as he imagined Nathan sitting there, night after night, reading by the lamp beside the chair. There was even a book on the little table.

On a shelf above the bed a row of strange looking objects attracted Marley's attention. He picked up a snakeskin bag that jingled when he held it. He spilled its contents out on the bed, revealing thirty or so tiles, each a bright color and with a strange symbol. Next on the shelf sat a Ouija Board that snuggled next to a bright metal sphere. Three other objects completed the inventory: a pendulum, a Raggedy Ann doll, and a bright yellow crystal.

Shutting the door on the last Greenwell's death chamber, Marley continued his journey, opening the next door to find a pink tiled bathroom with porcelains from the 1940s, including toilet, sink, and claw-footed bathtub. His opening of the door stirred up a layer of dust that danced upon the sunset beam coming in through the soda-bottle glass.

He reached the final doorway and paused, surveying what he'd passed. There'd been rooms for Thomas, Daniel, and Nathan. That only left Bobby. When he touched the doorknob, an electric shock traveled through his body and he imagined he heard a loud scream coming from downstairs. The door was locked, and no turning of the knob or pushing on the boards let him into that room.

# Chapter 6

Dusk had fallen, and back downstairs he found that the light coming in through the dilapidated curtains provided minimal illumination. Pushing the grate out of the way, he laid his sleeping bag out on the bed of the fireplace and applied the insect spray around the hearth's opening to keep out the night bugs and rodents. Laying his head down on his backpack, he soon fell sound asleep.

Marley startled awake to a strange howling sound. Checking his watch, he read a few minutes before midnight. He crawled out of his bag and flipped on his flashlight, watching a rat and a half dozen cockroaches scurry away. Following the howl towards the kitchen, he discovered the noise came from the grate he'd left open on the stove, allowing air to rush in and cause the strange noise. He latched it shut and headed back to his bed.

He'd just settled deep into his sleeping bag again when he heard a clattering coming from the kitchen. He made his way back in and flashed his light on the cooking pans. Several of them were swinging gently and one hook was empty. Sweeping the light on the floor, he discovered the missing pan on the floor. Picking it up, he found that it had a huge dent right in the middle of it. He snapped a photo.

Marley placed the dented pan on the counter and moved his light around, landing it on the knife rack. There he realized another knife was missing, a large cleaver, the type of tool used to chop through bone. Marley grabbed one of the other large knives for his own use, just in case, and headed back to his bed.

He'd just gotten back into his sleeping bag when he heard the sound of someone walking across the solid wooden floors above him.

He crawled out of bed, grabbing his flashlight in one hand and the knife in the other, and clumped up the stairs. Halfway up he called out, "Whoever's there, you better not cause any trouble. I'm armed."

He reached the top of the stairs just in time to see a flickering light go into the bedroom at the far end of the hall. Hurrying down the hallway, he was surprised to find this last door which had been securely locked was now partially open.

"Hello?" he called, letting the silence extend for a minute before pushing the door open the rest of the way. His flashlight showed him a bedroom similar to the one he'd labeled Daniel's with a single bed, armoire, and dresser. He took a step in and stood, pointing his flashlight in various corners.

For a moment Marley felt dizzy. He blinked, and when he opened his eyes the room had changed. It was now clean and bright, oil lamps burning and a clean breeze drifting in through the window, its bright curtains fluttering. A young man sat on the small dressing chair, a black man combing his hair.

The man stood and he and the servant walked right through Marley, creating a tingling through his body, and continued out the door. Marley followed them and watched them drift through the bathroom door. When Marley stepped in, he found the room wasn't the bathroom he'd just seen, but rather a more ancient one, with a metal sink and a pot without a toilet. Water was dripping, a moist towel hung on the rack, and shaving cream sat in a container next to a straight razor.

Marley blinked again and found himself back in the bathroom with the pink tiles and toilet, dry and dark. No shaving cream or razor sat by the sink, no towel hung on the rack, no water dripped from the dry faucet.

Marley headed back into the hallway and wriggled his nose. He followed the smell of cigar smoke to the beginning of the hall, to the first room he'd explored earlier. Pushing the door open and shining his flashlight around, he saw a spirit sitting in one of the large chairs, reading a book, a cigar in his hand. When he raised his phone to take a picture, the image disappeared.

After several minutes passed and no further signs of haunting appeared, Marley returned to his sleeping bag, snuggling in and staring at the top of the fireplace.

"Well, I certainly proved one thing tonight," he muttered. "This mansion really is haunted. What a nice story this is going to be for the evening news."

# Chapter 7

In the morning, Marley awoke to the song of a bird who'd made its nest on top of one of the paintings. A ray of sunshine flickered through a tear in one of the curtains. He stepped out the front door to relieve himself, enjoying the beautiful dawn, the sun just rising over the tall brick fence and lighting up the dilapidated porch. Settling onto the top step, he ate the fruit and water he'd brought as he listened to the morning birds.

"I guess the wildlife isn't afraid of ghosts, so I shouldn't be either," he said.

He decided he'd check out the kitchen again and, stepping in, was astonished to see that all the pans hung in their proper place, including the one that had the dent during the night, although now it looked unblemished. On the knife rack the cleaver held its proper spot, with the only two empty spaces the old one and where he'd taken his weapon. He returned that knife to its spot. For just a moment he wondered if he'd dreamt all of the previous night's activity, then shook his head, certain he could tell the difference between dreams and reality. Besides, he had the photo of the dented pot on his camera.

He climbed back upstairs and found everything as it had been the previous evening, including Bobby's door securely locked.

Back downstairs, Marley packed up the cedar box into his backpack along with his other supplies and rolled up his sleeping bag. He took one last look around the grand room, imagining the great parties and dinners once held here, the people dancing in their antebellum outfits, and the hopes and dreams of Thomas' Southern empire. Closing the front door behind him, he made his way back out the weed invaded front yard. When he reached the iron gate it seemed to open on its own.

Over breakfast at Mabel's, Allie listened spellbound as Marley related all that had happened.

"See! I TOLD you it was haunted," she said.

"Indeed," he agreed. "We need to find out more about the brother, Bobby. Since the ghost was in his room, it might have been his. We already discovered that he disappeared soon after returning from the war."

"Maybe he just got tired of arguing with his brother and headed back North to be with people whose philosophy he agreed with," Allie suggested.

Marley shrugged. "I suppose that's possible. Still, I'm thinking that body behind the fireplace is his. He might have died from natural causes or an accident, medicine offered little aid in those days. I have to wonder, if it is his, why was he buried there and not in a graveyard? In fact, where are all the Greenwell bodies? Only Nathan is buried in the local cemetery."

Allie looked around the café before leaning in to whisper, "You're thinking that Daniel killed his brother and buried him in that tomb, then boarded up the entry behind the fireplace, aren't you? I bet it's Bobby's ghost haunting the mansion."

"Yes, that's my current theory." Marley finished off his eggs while he considered. "Why were there two ghosts? Why is there a servant hanging around? And what about the mysteries of the missing knives and disarrayed pans?"

"Tell me again about the ghost in the sitting room."

"Not much to tell. The shadow was quite vague, just a cigar smoker. That old house could have lots of ghosts I suppose."

He quieted as Mabel came up to refill their coffee cups and clear away the empty plates.

"I gotta admit I was wrong about you, Mr. Robbins," she said.

"How so?"

"I never figured you to amount to anything. Those first few shows when all you were coming up with was local gossip, well, I guess that was sort of interesting too. But those reports you've been making about the old Greenwell Mansion have got the town buzzing. You two thinking of buying the old place and fixin' it up? Could be made into a museum or something."

Marley and Allie stared at each other.

"Um... well, we hadn't actually thought about it."

"No?" Mabel snorted. "I could just see you two there, two fuddy-duddy nerds in an old dilapidated haunted house. Ha ha! Seems perfect to me!" She wandered away, chuckling to herself.

"Buy it?" Allie grasped her napkin in her hands. "Oh, Marley! Do you think we could? Wouldn't that be just heavenly? I mean, we'd have to get rid of the ghosts first, but if we could, can you just imagine? That big old historic place all fixed up?"

"Just wait 'til you see it inside! It's incredible! Look at these photos. Carved staircases, crystal chandeliers, and a humongous dining table. All the upholstery, drapes, and curtains are ruined by age, of course."

The two ogled over the photos as they sipped their coffee. Allie pointed out some of the artifacts, telling where they had come from, while Marley made comments about the occupants' lifestyles, based on his deductions from the details of pictures and furniture placement.

"Oh, I'd love to have this house," Allie said, her heart aflutter. "What do you think it would take?"

"Let's find out!"

At the courthouse the next morning Marley was told that the city had taken possession of the property for unpaid taxes. The official there informed him that for $40,000 in back taxes he could own the property, including all the furnishings.

"Before we decide to buy it, I've got to see the insides for myself," Allie said. Marley agreed, and that afternoon, right after their tapings, she drove them back to the mansion for Allie's first look inside.

Once on the porch, Allie stood outside the front door hugging herself tightly.

"Come on," Marley said, trying to loosen the grip she had on herself. "The ghosts only come out at night."

"Well ... if you're sure." She let him lead her into the house and one step in she stopped still, her jaw falling open. "Why ... why ... it's even more fantastic than in your pictures! Look at that chandelier. All the antique furnishings. Oh, and the fireplace, wow, wow, wow!"

For four hours she walked all over the house, taking two hundred photos on her cell phone. She swooned at the huge displays of cooking and dining pieces.

"If we ever should get this house," she said, "I'd want to modernize the kitchen. You do know I'm a pretty good cook, huh?"

Marley grinned widely. "Don't forget you've been sharing your leftovers with yours truly for the past three weeks. Since only you and your Dad live in the house, I figured it likely that you were the cook. And, of course, you're always looking up recipes in magazines and online."

Together they went room by room, sketching out the floor plan, upstairs and down.

"How would we ever restore all this?" she asked. "It's going to take months and a bucket of money. How much cash do you have?"

"I'm barely making my school debt payments, rent, and food with the pittance I'm earning from Mr. Cohen," he admitted. "I guess if we can buy it, I could live here and save my rent payments." He flicked a spider off the arm of one of the chairs. "How about you?"

"I've got just over a thousand dollars in the bank. Maybe we could sell a few of the mansion's pieces and use that money for restoration," Allie suggested. "I know an antique dealer in Atlanta – we could send him pictures of some of the furniture and see what he suggests."

"Yeah, maybe. But we can't do that until we come up with the $40,000 in advance. I don't see a bank loaning us that much money."

They looked at each other sadly until Allie's eyes brightened. "Say, didn't you say you'd found some old coins in the house? My dad collects coins. Maybe he'll loan us the money based on those coins and these pictures I've taken."

"Great! I've been wanting to meet your father and see where you live. Maybe I can get a home cooked meal out of this deal, too."

"Oh, you'll love my dad. Everyone does. Got a heart of gold."

# Chapter 8

"So, you're the young man my Allison's been ragging on about?"

"Dad!"

Mr. Burton chuckled. Mostly balding, with only a monk's rim of hair over his ears and around the back of his skull, his jolly face glowed around his sparkling eyes and heavy jowls. Sitting behind his big desk, he reached forward to shake Marley's hand.

"I must say," he continued, "you're the first fellow Allison's showed the least interest in during her twenty-two years. I can see you're just as nerdy as she is."

"Dad!" she shouted again. "If you're going to be rude, we'll just leave."

He laughed out loud. "Okay, okay. Sorry Little Doe." He turned to Marley. "I call her Little Doe. Did she tell you that?"

Marley shook his head. "We're just friends, sir. In fact, we've only known each other for three weeks."

"Doesn't take long to fall in love, now does it?"

"I said we're just friends, sir."

He chuckled. "Yes, I heard you. So, what can I do for you, young fellow?"

Marley pulled the bag out of his pocket and handed it across the desk. "We were wondering if you'd take a look at these coins I have. I'm in need of some money and Allie said you might tell us what they're worth."

The older man glanced into the bag and both eyebrows arched. Pulling over a large lighted magnifying stand from the corner of his desk, he extracted one coin with padded forceps and examined both sides carefully. He turned to his computer and scrolled through some screens.

Turning to Marley he asked, "Where did you get these?"

"Well, I ..."

Allie interrupted, "He inherited them from his grandfather. They've been in the family a long time. Are they valuable?"

Mr. Burton put the first coin down and pulled out another one, also looking it up on the computer after he'd identified it. He proceeded to pull them out one at a time, jotting notes on a pad with figures after each one before setting it down, building an array of two rows of ten.

"Young man, you have a small fortune here. This first one, a 1910-D ten-dollar Indian Eagle is worth about $4500. This second one, a 1907 twenty-dollar Saint Gaudens, should fetch upwards of $2500. Based on my evaluations, I'd say this bag might be worth upwards of $50,000."

Marley swallowed hard, too stunned to speak. Reaching up, he puffed out the hair behind his left ear before he finally squeaked out. "Sir. Could you take these as collateral and loan me $40,000? Then you could sell them for me."

Mr. Burton looked from Marley to Allie and then back again. "Yes, I suppose so. Why?"

Marley glanced at Allie who indicated that he should answer.

"It's like this, sir," Marley said. "We, that is, Allie and I, we're thinking of buying a house together. You know, an investment."

Mr. Burton sat back in his chair, his hands grasped together in his lap. "Really, now. You two claim to just be friends and yet you're talking about putting a down payment on a home, huh? Well, young love can be impetuous I suppose. Where are you looking? That new subdivision north of town, what's it called, 'The Oaks'?"

"Actually, sir, the $40,000 is the total selling price. We're looking at the old Greenwell Mansion. We can get it for past taxes."

Thumbing his fingers against the desk, Mr. Burton stared at his daughter. "The old Greenwell Mansion huh? That place has been neglected for forty years. It must be a total wreck. Before you invest in such a place, you'd want to go inspect it from the inside ..."

He paused and looked at the coins again. "From your grandfather, huh? Well, I guess I'd better not ask any more questions. Okay, you want to risk $40,000 and your reputation on an old fixer-upper ... why not? I'll come with you now to the courthouse and see if we can sign the papers."

# Chapter 9

Allie came out with the spaghetti and meatball dish she'd prepared, and everyone took a helping. After a prayer they dug in, Marley clearly relishing the home cooking. He had thirds.

"I used to be able to eat like that," Mr. Burton said with a sigh.

"And look where it got you." Allie pointed to her father's stomach. "Don't you even think about seconds."

"Don't be a young whippersnapper, Little Doe. Don't forget I just helped you buy a house."

Allie kissed his cheek. "Oh, yes. Thanks again, Dad. Really, I still can't believe it's ours! All that historic data and valuable antiques! It's an amazing buy."

"Yep, the whole kit and caboodle," Marley replied. He looked over at Mr. Burton who gave him a wink.

"Now you'll just have to figure out how you're going to be able to afford to restore and maintain it," Mr. Burton said. "Or maybe you'll just want to strip the insides and level the place."

Marley shook his head vigorously. "Oh no, Mr. Burton. We plan to fix it up and live there the rest of our lives."

After the dishes were put away, Allie loaded her cell phone photos onto her laptop and the three of them studied the pictures. They tried to price some of the items online, but the condition of the pieces made their job difficult.

"I think your idea of getting professional assessors involved is a good one," Mr. Burton noted.

He suggested they make a list of what needed to be done to make the place livable. On top of the list were the desperate repairs, like fixing all the broken windows, putting on a new roof, hiring an exterminator, and cleaning out all the ruined carpets and drapes. Then came the major installations, like plumbing, electricity, insulation, and gutters. Allie reminded him that she needed an updated kitchen, and he put that next. It seemed like furnishings would have to wait.

Mr. Burton wondered whether it would be worth seeing if the house could be made into a historic landmark. He helped them look up the procedures to apply for the designation, and then searched for corporations that would donate money to rebuild those types of places. Allie promised to fill out the grant applications.

The Atlanta antique dealer replied to Allie's email promptly and said he could come down Saturday, in two days. He arrived at nine, and spent several hours touring the home, carefully inspecting several of the pieces that had interested him in the photos Allie had sent him. The antique draperies, he reported, were ruined and should be scrapped. Most of the carpets had been destroyed by the rodents. However, the furniture could be reupholstered, and several were collector items, including various items in the kitchen and bedrooms, particularly some of the antique armoires and cedar chests. He gave Allie a list of twelve furniture items he thought might fetch the most money, ranging in value from two to fifteen thousand dollars. He also gave her a price list for reupholstering, which would be required before any of the chairs could be sold. By far, the most valuable pieces were the gold frames around the photographs. At the current price of gold, the fourteen frames would fetch between $3000 and $20,000 each, based on their weight. In addition, he recommended that the jewelry be appraised as individual pieces by a specialist he knew in Atlanta named Roger Striker. He suggested that when they were ready, they could bring the pieces up.

Marley and Allie were delighted! They chose to sell three of the frames bringing in five thousand dollars so they could get a start on the house's restoration. It quickly became apparent that this wouldn't be sufficient, and piece by piece over the next few weeks they sold another frame and once a piece of furniture to pay their contractors.

As the workers redid the electricity, plumbing, windows, carpentry, and roofing, the two spent every spare hour cleaning their home. Allie selected the new appliances to be installed in the kitchen and bathrooms, as well as the new fixtures and drapes to go throughout the house.

On his evening television show, Marley devoted fifteen minutes of his broadcast to the house and the progress he and Allie were making, using videos they created with the studio's equipment. On each segment, he discussed a bit about the mansion's history, how the repairs were progressing, and some of the pieces they'd discovered. Mr. Cohen was delighted with the enthusiasm the show had generated in town, bringing him advertisements from local dealers. He was able to give both Allie and Marley raises.

# Chapter 10

One evening, sitting together at Allie's kitchen table, they opened the small cedar box Marley had brought back that first day. Inside, they found stacks of letters tied in ribbons. There were five bundles, each from a different correspondent.

The first stack was a set written from Sarah to Thomas. Allie and Marley giggled as they read the formalized communication, not the kind of love notes that normally would pass between happily married couples. On the one about Daniel's birth, for example, she had printed his tiny fingerprints on the bottom of the page, documenting his vital statistics of birth, weight, height, and time of birth. She said he was a fussy baby and commented on the slave nursemaid she was using for his breast feeding. There were no words of endearment in the letter, either to her husband or about her baby. The one about Bobby's birth was different. Although it too had his fingerprints and birth facts, it had a more loving tone, describing him as a sweet and lovable child.

The next stack they went through was from a cousin from Virginia. Daniel and he had corresponded off and on over the years, and according to the letters, twice he'd visited, once in 1858 when George was twenty-one and on his honeymoon on a tour of the South, and then ten years later, when Daniel was in the midst of supporting the town of Greenwell. The last letter read as follows.

28 October, 1868.

Dear Daniel,

Let me express again my appreciation for the wonderful hosting you provided Kathleen and I this summer. Those evenings on the veranda with the mint julips will forever be in our memories. It's good to see that the old time South has not completely disappeared off the face of this once great nation.

I again apologize for my wife's persistence in asking about Bobby. She apologizes as well and repeats she didn't mean to offend you and only asked because she had met him on our first visit.

She also tells me that she talked to that servant Olive you provided me for the night. That nigger said that the old family servant, Joseph, disappeared the same weekend as did Bobby. Kathleen had been very impressed with Joseph and how devoted he was to your family. She wanted me to ask, if the question won't offend you, if you think they ran away together? You know how she is with the family tree, always trying to fill in the details.

Again, we offer great appreciation for your kind hosting and would be delighted to return the favor if you should ever find the time to come Virginia way.

Sincerely,

Your cousins, George and Kathleen Kirkpatrick


A few days later, during the refurbishing of the kitchen, the plumber asked Marley about access through the basement.

"Basement?"

The plumber explained, "The original pipes from the sink seem to dip into a space below the house, and I can feel a musty cold coming in around them, so I assume

you gotta have a basement or at least a crawlspace. I
don't know how to access it, though. Sometimes in these
old houses there's a trapdoor in the pantry."

After the workmen had left for the day, Marley
went into the pantry that still held shelves of old mason
jars. When he moved toward the back of the closet, he
felt some of the floorboards shifting under his feet and,
pulling them away, discovered a large metal hatch
covering an opening to a cellar. He descended carefully,
the old wooden ladder inside creaking with each step.

The musty cellar was about ten feet deep, 20 by
40 feet in size, with a dirt floor. Without a single window
for ventilation, Marley's flashlight provided the only
illumination. As he stepped around the room, he noticed
that the ground was mostly firm underfoot, but softer in
places. Each time he stepped on a soft area, he imagined
he could hear a faint moan.

Along the walls, Marley discovered deteriorated
nameplates hammered into the brick, one positioned at
the end of each soft spot. One held the name Sarah, and
he realized this must be Sarah Greenwell's grave,
Thomas' wife. Most of the other plates were too rusted
to read, but the last one shined in his light, seemingly

untouched by age. In proud justified letters, he read "Joseph."

"He must have been very highly thought of, indeed, to be buried in the family tomb," he whispered.

# Chapter 11

By the end of two months, the house had been stripped of all the moldy curtains and carpets, the hardwood floors polished, electricity wired, plumbing piped, a new roof shingled, air conditioning installed, and broken windows replaced.

One night after dinner at Allie's, Marley told her he was ready to move permanently into the house.

"Are you sure you want to spend the nights there with those ghosts?" Allie asked him, holding both his hands in a vise-like grip.

"I gotta," he said. "I can't keep paying rent and, well, the ghosts aren't going to hurt me after all."

"Okay, let me give you a kiss for luck." She bent forward and kissed him on the cheek, and Marley felt himself blush.

"You know, I really like you," he told her.

She laughed. "I could tell. I really like you, too! Maybe someday we'll do something more than have chaste kisses, you think?"

She drove him to the mansion's property, and he waved at her from that old iron gate, watching her wave back and then drive away. The sun had just set and the night owl had begun its hooting. Marley walked into the house and flipped on the living room light, admiring how nice the room looked, open and airy, with the two refurbished chairs and table set up in front of the fireplace. He turned off the light and climbed the polished staircase to his room, the one which had once been Thomas and Sarah Greenwell's so many years ago. He'd retained all the old furniture, the armoire, dresser, and bed frame, adding a new mattress and a small end table with a lamp and alarm clock. He showered and brushed his teeth, and then tucked himself into the fresh cotton sheets, smiling to himself at the success he and Allie had made of refurbishing the home.

About midnight, Marley was awakened by the sound of footsteps on the creaking floor in the hallway. He grabbed his flashlight and listened at his bedroom door. Looking down, he saw a flickering light coming from the opening below his door. He jumped into the hallway, and looking down towards the far end, saw a lamp emitting a hazy dismal type of light. It seemed to be dancing from one bedroom doorway to another.

"Who's there?" Marley shouted.

No answer came, but the lamp seemed to melt into the doorway at the end of the hall, the room that used to be Bobby's. When he reached it, he saw a faint light coming from beneath the crack at the bottom of the door. From inside the room he heard a faint singing, a melody like one of the old slave songs. In moments both the singing and the light faded away. He opened the door and turned on the overhead light, finding the room empty, just as it had been when he last saw it.

He turned off the light and headed back to his own bed, snuggling into the still warm sheets. He wondered who could be the ghost and why was he haunting the mansion? He soon fell asleep, dreaming of ghosts and Civil War heroes.

At the studio the next morning, Allie was waiting eagerly for Marley to come in and tell how his night in the mansion had gone.

"Did you see any ghosts?" she demanded.

"Well, maybe." He told her about the sound of footsteps in the hallway, the flickering light that disappeared into Bobby's room, and the singing he'd heard. Just as he was finishing, a knock came at the studio's door

She gave him a mischievous smile. "I have a surprise for you."

He raised an eyebrow. "Yeah?"

She rushed over to the door and opened it to reveal a short thin man with a bushy black beard. He wore a black trench coat and a strange black hat covering unruly gray hair.

He followed her over to where Marley was standing and held out his hand.

"Marley, let me introduce you to Mr. Simone Gartham. Simone, this is Marley Robbins."

"Pleasure to meet you," the fellow said, shaking Marley's hand vigorously. "I've been following your reports about the Greenwell Mansion, hoping we'd get a chance to talk."

Marley nodded. "You're into the occult, Mr. Gartham? A ghost hunter I would say."

The fellow stepped back, a surprised look to his eyes. "Call me Simone. Allie must have told you about me, huh?"

Marley shook his head. "No. I noticed the occult pentagram necklace you're wearing, the EMF meter on your belt, and the ghostbuster tattoo on your left wrist."

Simone laughed. "Very observant, young man. Allie invited me to film for your show, talking with you about ghosts."

Allie helped set up the studio and cameras for the filming, and the two settled into chairs in front of the green screen. After the usual introduction material, including the local police report and weather, they had a talk about ghosts.

"The main thing I want to know," Marley said, "is why the house is being haunted. What makes a ghost?"

Simone stroked his beard, considering his answer carefully. "There can be different reasons, such as guarding a treasure, an unfinished mission, or searching for something valuable they lost, particularly a child. But by far the most common reason is that the person was murdered in the home and the murderer was never punished."

"You've mentioned different ways of getting rid of ghosts," Marley said, "like burning sage and using holy water. Would that work for ghosts looking for revenge?"

"No. When the ghost represents an unsolved murder victim, the only way to release them from their hauntings is to reveal the murderer, and then rebury the bodies with a proper funeral."

That afternoon, as Marley sat working at the old rolltop desk, he noticed an envelope crunched up in a cubbyhole. He squinted at it, pretty sure it hadn't been there before, but unsure if maybe he had just overlooked it. Pulling and straightening it out, he found that it was an old Western Union Telegraph, still sealed. Inside he found an original teletype, just like the kind used in the 1800s. There was no date on the sheet, merely the words "Please bring him to justice."

He wondered if maybe he'd brought it in with some other papers from the mail and had absent-mindedly stuck it in that slot. Looking up the number on the Internet, he called the local Western Union office and asked if they had delivered a telegram to his house over the past few days. They assured him that they had no record of the transaction and, furthermore, Western Union had discontinued delivering telegraph messages in 2006.

Chapter 12

The next weekend came their scheduled trip to
Atlanta. Allie had made reservations for two rooms at the
Holiday Inn and they each brought an overnight bag. Allie
picked out three pieces of the jewelry from the house to
bring to the appraiser and they got an early start. It was
only a four-hour drive, and they talked non-stop the
whole way. They shared so many interests, such as
history, journalism, and the house, that the trip seemed
to fly by.

Their first stop was at Roger Striker's shop, the
jeweler who specialized in estate pieces. Allie handed him
the three pieces in a velvet bag, and the jeweler took
them out one at a time, examining each carefully.

"One of the ways to estimate the value of jewelry
is by the type of mounting used for the piece," the
jeweler explained. He showed the couple where to look
with the magnifying glass to read the symbol designating
the gold purity. One stamp read "18k," the other two
"24k."

"As you can imagine, each piece's value is based
not only on its precious metal content, but also on its
artistic value and history. This one, for example," he

picked up a green stoned ring, "this Early Georgian turquois ring with a solid gold intricate weaving would probably fetch about $1500 at most auctions. This one, what I'd describe as a black topaz crowned heart betrothal ring with foil wrappings and diamond chips, probably dates from about 1800. I'd estimate its value at about $1300. As you might have guessed, by far the most valuable is this Tahitian cultured pearl and diamond necklace strung on white gold. The alternating color scheme of these pearls is mesmerizing. I guess this one would top $30,000 in the right market."

"What would you give us for them?" Allie asked.

The jeweler stroked his chin, looking at the jewelry, then at Allie, and then back at the jewelry. "Well, I can give you 50% of my valuation for the two rings. That'd be $1400. The necklace is a bit beyond my operating expenses at the moment. I'll be happy to hold it and try to sell it for you for a 40% commission. Would you like to do that?"

Allie nodded. "Yes, that would be great!"

"Fourteen hundred dollars in cash! We're rich!" Marley exclaimed. He grabbed Allie and gave her a long, deep kiss. He had never done this before, but she didn't seem to mind so he kept on kissing.

Roger waited until they were done and cleared his throat.

Looking over at him, Allie said, "Oh, you look worried. What's wrong?"

Roger bit his lip. "I don't mean to pry into your personal business, but selling your antique jewelry might be something you'll regret later. You'll never be able to replace these pieces."

Allie gave a light laugh. "We still have plenty more at home."

"And when you've sold them all, then what?"

Allie and Marley looked at each other. "Well, I guess we'll have to figure out some other way to make money," she said.

Walking out with her purse and his wallet both bulging with cash, worries about the future quickly fluttered away. They picked one of the fanciest restaurants in town and enjoyed a scrumptious meal before heading to their hotel. The check-in line was long and it took almost forty-minutes before they got their turn at the front desk.

"Reservation under Allie Burton," she told the desk clerk.

He looked up her reservation and copied her license and credit card information. Handing her a card key, the clerk said, "Room 312. Good thing you got here before ten, otherwise we'd have released your room. It's the last one we've got."

Allie looked at the key, then up at the clerk, then back at Marley, and then back to the clerk. "There's only one key? I distinctly made reservations for two rooms."

The clerk checked the computer again. "Nope. Says here one room for two people. Sorry about that. You know this weekend both the Falcons and the Braves are playing, don't you? I doubt if you'll find another available room for a forty-mile radius."

Allie told Marley the news and the two of them went up to the room to look it over. It was a typical small hotel room, a single king bed with hardly a foot of space on either side. A small desk and chair hugged the wall next to a dresser that had a flat screen TV against the wall.

"I could sleep in the car?" Marley offered.

"Don't be silly. This bed's plenty big enough for the both of us."

He smiled shyly. "Well, if you don't mind, okay I guess. You know I'm a gentleman."

"Sometimes too much!" she said, stomping her foot.

He looked at her a bit confused, until she took his head in both hands, drawing it down to kiss him fully on the mouth. He kissed her back, and soon they found that a bed half that size still would have been big enough for them both.

## Chapter 13

The next morning over breakfast, Marley held her hand as they ate.

"You know, the house is really big."

She sipped her coffee, looking at him from under her bangs. "Yes, that's true."

"Lots of bedrooms."

"Uh-huh."

He sighed, finishing off his scrambled eggs and starting on his toast. He threw it back onto the plate. "Look, what I'm trying to say is that maybe you should think about moving into the mansion, too. You know, to save rent and maybe so I'm not alone at night."

Allie picked up his hand and kissed it. "Hush, you silly shy man. Of course, I'd love to live with you. As soon as we get back, I'll pack up my stuff and, no, I won't need my own bedroom. I think we proved last night that one bed is sufficient for the two of us. There is one condition, though. You have to promise to protect me from the ghosts."

Marley gave her a big kiss. "You bet! They only come out at night and I'll be there by your side!"

They continued talking about their Atlanta adventure as they sipped their after-breakfast coffee.

"You know, we have a lot of very valuable items in the house. Once we get back, we should purchase a safe to store the more valuable keepsakes."

They did just that, and placed in all the house jewelry, securely locking it up. The next day Allie asked him to open it again to place her mother's wedding ring that she'd brought from home. When he opened it, the two were startled to find a telegram from Western Union sitting inside on top of the jewelry. Just like the first one there was a one-line teletyped message. This time it read, "My bones protect."

"What do you think it means?" Allie asked.

"Clearly there's something to do with bones. Maybe the ones in the family crypt in the cellar?"

"You said you think one of the ghosts might be that of the servant Joseph," Allie said. "Is that because both Bobby and he disappeared from the house at about the same time?"

"Yes, there's that. And one of the ghosts I saw seemed to be African American. But I was thinking about another strange thing. The first time I came into the house everything was covered in layers of dust –

everything, that is, except for the pots and knives in the kitchen and the handrails on the staircase. I'm wondering if Joseph, as family servant, didn't continue to take care of those things even after death."

Allie squinted at him. "That's pretty far-fetched."

"Hey, you're the one who believed in ghosts first! Anyway, yeah, I think Joseph is one of the ghosts. If this message refers to him, I guess we should go see what's in his crypt."

"Really? You want to go graverobbing?" Allie asked, her eyes large.

Marley shrugged. "I guess that's pretty gruesome, huh? You don't want to have any part of it?"

"Are you kidding? I can hardly wait. This is a part of archeology I never got to try. Let's borrow lights from the studio so we can light up that cellar. Drop a couple of shovels and bring a more reliable ladder, okay? Oh, and we'll need gloves and masks."

It took them a couple of hours to get it all set up. Marley fixed the twelve-foot aluminum ladder so that it made a secure access to the basement and lowered the two shovels. He dropped down an extension cord and, once on the ground inside, set up three bright lights they'd borrowed from the studio.

They found Joseph's grave at the corner of the room and the two of them began digging. It took half an hour to scrape out the dirt and reveal the wooden coffin, the top of which gave way to a sharp blow from Marley's shovel. They pulled out the wooden pieces and found a set of desiccated human bones. Focusing their lights inside the coffin, they saw something shiny in the middle of the skeleton's chest. Allie reached down into the coffin and pulled out the object. They both gasped, recognizing its identity immediately. It was the missing kitchen knife.

"Do you think...?"

Allie cocked her head at Marley. "What?"

"Well," he continued, "I'm just wondering if one could get fingerprints off a knife that's been buried for a hundred and fifty years. Do you remember what that ghost hunter said? Gartham was his name wasn't it? He said if the murderer could be revealed and the body reburied, that would put the ghost to rest."

"Hey, it's worth a try!"

Allie placed the knife in a plastic bag and the next morning contacted Detective Drake, the city's police detective. He followed them down to inspect the graves and then sat at the kitchen table with them, examining the knife.

"Families sometimes buried their loved ones in cellars in those days," Drake explained. "It was to protect them from grave robbers. I could ask the state forensics to get involved if you want. As far as fingerprints, though, our records only go back fifty years. You'd have to have a set of the fingerprints of the suspected killer so we'd have something to compare these with."

Allie's eyes lit up. "We DO have a set of his fingerprints ... well, a set of fingerprints from the person we suspect did the murders." She turned to Marley. "Go get the stack of letters from Sarah we went through."

He smiled. "Right. One of them had a set of Daniel's fingerprints as an infant." He asked the detective if that would do and Drake said it would.

When Marley got back with the letter, he said there might be a second murder too. He didn't want to go into details yet, but if they found another weapon, could they call him back? With assurances that they could, Detective Drake left with the knife and a photograph of the fingerprinted letter.

"You're thinking those are Bobby's bones behind the fireplace, aren't you?" Allie asked.

"Yep! You up for another round of gravedigging?"

She gave him a huge grin. "You bet! Let's go for it."

Removing the grate, Marley crawled into the back of the fireplace carrying a hammer and chisel. He'd had one of the repairmen plaster the inside, so it took him nearly an hour to break that out and remove the bricks wide enough to again gain entry to the tomb. He crawled through the hole and then took in and set up the light that she fed him. Its stark slate luminescence created a ghostly shimmer in the room. He then helped Allie wiggle in.

She looked around, astounded. "Wow! I mean, we've discovered lots of little hiding places all over this house. Remember the one in the upstairs sitting room that held all those old bottles of liquor behind the portrait? But, really, how did we miss this huge place when we sketched out the floor plans?"

"One of the many great advantages of having a creepy old mansion to explore." Marley pulled at the tuft of hair behind his ear as he surveyed the space. "After we move Bobby's bones out, I think this place would be a great wine cellar."

She stepped over and kissed him, something they'd been doing a lot of since their Atlanta trip. "As usual, you're so right!"

Putting on their gloves, they lifted the lid off the sarcophagus and lowered the marble slab to the floor. Inside, the sword glimmered in the reflected light. Lifting it carefully, they discovered that the hilt had a set of easily distinguishable bloody fingerprints, preserved against deterioration in the tomb. In addition, the blade had a dark crimson stain, clearly blood.

"So, Daniel used this sword to kill his brother, and then buried it with him in the fireplace. Wow."

Allie picked up the skull. "Look here. There's a big crack across the skull. It looks like it was smashed with something."

Marley's eyes widened. "Oh! Remember me telling you about my first night in the house? I found a large pan on the kitchen floor with a big round dent in the middle. I get it now. The ghosts were telling me that's how Daniel killed Bobby. He smashed in his head with the pan, and then stabbed him with his sword. Joseph must have tried to stop him, so Daniel grabbed a kitchen knife and killed him too!"

"Poor Bobby."

"And, hey, look at Bobby's right forearm bones. They're sliced through. That's why the cleaver was missing that first night I stayed here. Daniel must have chopped through Bobby's arm to get the sword. Hmm. I can picture the whole fight in my mind."

Allie shivered. "No wonder the house is haunted! Well, once we turn this sword over to Detective Drake we'll have proof that Daniel killed these two. We can arrange for their proper burial and then the ghosts won't come back." She noticed that Marley's attention was focused on the inside of the coffin. "Something else wrong?"

Reaching around the body and under the bottom of the muslin shroud, Marley scooped out a piece of glittering metal. Showing it to Allie she let out a loud whistle. "A gold bar! Look, it has the stamp of the Confederacy!"

Carefully moving Bobby's bones aside, they lifted the edge of the muslin to reveal that the bottom of the tomb was lined with what seemed like scores, maybe even a couple of hundred similar gold bars.

"Daniel must have brought these back from the war and buried them here. Marley, oh Marley, we're rich beyond our wildest dreams!"

# Chapter 14

Over supper that evening, the two toasted their new found wealth with a delicious wine Marley had bought, along with the roast chicken Allie prepared. They feasted, talking about how wonderfully happy they were.

"You know," Allie said, "there're still a lot of mysteries we haven't solved about this house."

"Oh? How's that?"

"Well, for one thing, we still don't know why Nathan was such a hermit. Why are there no pictures of him anywhere? Why is it he made sure no one ever saw him his entire life? Do you suppose he was incredibly deformed or something?"

Marley chuckled. "You haven't figured that out yet, huh? Seems pretty obvious to me."

Allie waited for a minute, but as he continued to sit back looking smug, she picked up a fork full of mashed potatoes and flung it at him. He swatted it away just in time.

"Tell me!"

He chuckled. "So, we know that Daniel never married, and the Greenwells were known to dabble with the servants. It seems obvious to me that Nathan was the result of one of Daniel's dalliances with an African-American. He decided to adopt the child and make him his heir, but he didn't want the town seeing that he had a half black child. He sent the boy off to Europe, and Nathan was perfectly happy to spend the rest of his life there, away from his mean father and the bigoted attitudes in Greenwell. When he had to come back, he chose to never let it be known he was a mulatto by never letting anyone but his servant see him. The servant was able to keep the secret, and so it died with Nathan's death."

"You are so clever, Marley. That's one of the reasons I love you so much." She kissed him again. "Anything else you haven't told me about Nathan?"

"Yep. Remember those strange objects on the shelf over his bed?"

"You mean the Ouija board and all that?"

"Exactly. Those are ways of communicating with ghosts. He had a bag with runes, too. Clearly, he was aware of the hauntings. I guess we'll never know if he actually communicated with them."

"Ooh," Allie whistled. "I bet we have even more mysteries to uncover."

After dinner, Allie and Marley were doing the dishes when Allie heard a strange moaning coming from the cellar.

"Do you hear that?" she asked.

"What?"

"Something coming from the cellar. Listen. Don't you hear it?"

Marley stood listening, and then shook his head. "I don't hear anything."

"Well I do, and I'm going to investigate."

Taking a flashlight, she climbed down the ladder that Marley had left in place and, reaching the ground, realized that the eerie moan came from one of the graves. As she stood immediately over the located grave, the ground began to slowly sink. She stepped onto a firm part of the floor, watching as the grave sank about 12 inches. With each inch the moaning grew louder.

"Oh, spirit from the past," Allie called, "Do you have a message for me?"

The walls of the dark room shook. Pointing her flashlight beam directly toward the grave, she saw a sparkle reflected in her light. She knelt and picked up a magnificently beautiful two-karat diamond solitaire ring.

When she slipped it onto her finger the eerie sounds ceased, and all was calm.

"Hey, everything all right down there?" Marley called from the hatch in the pantry.

She climbed back up and, taking off the ring, dropped it in his palm. As soon as it left her finger the moaning from the basement resumed.

"Clearly the spirits want me to wear this," she said, reaching for it.

But Marley held it back. Going down on one knee he said, "Allison Burton, will you do me the great honor of becoming my wife?"

Allie grabbed her love and planted a big loving kiss on his eager lips. "YES, YES, YES."

She held out her hand and he slipped the ring on, and the moaning from below stopped.

# Chapter 15

Detective Drake confirmed that the fingerprints
on the knife and sword were Daniel's. Marley's television
shows explaining how Daniel had murdered his brother
and servant were such great hits, they were picked up by
national television. He got a job in Montgomery at a
major affiliate as an investigative reporter.

Daniel's statue was taken down from the Town
Green and replaced with an obelisk commemorating the
slaves who died unheralded before 1860. All the graves in
the cellar were inspected by the county medical examiner
and an anthropologist from the State University said that
the youngest grave was at least 150 years old. The bones
of the deceased were dug up, including Bobby's from the
tomb, and all reinterred in the local cemetery with proper
ceremonies.

The gold bullion was sold, bringing in just over
eighteen million dollars that Allie's father helped them
invest properly, guaranteeing them to never have money
worries again. Once the mansion and grounds were
properly restored, Allie led visitors on tours, Wednesday
afternoons from 2 to 4, describing the many historic

items, photos, and period pieces, and the history of the house and area.

In June the two had a fabulous wedding, attended by everyone in town. Their life seemed ideal, although Marley often said he missed the excitement of ghost hunting.

# Epilogue

One day, two years later, Allie and Marley were enjoying their morning coffee and paper and Marley said, "You know, there's still another mystery we never solved."

"Oh?"

"Do you remember my telling about my first night in the mansion? I told you of seeing Bobby and Joseph's ghosts in his bedroom walking into the bathroom and disappearing?"

"Yes, I remember," she said. "That led to the whole adventure, of course. Now their souls are at rest and their bodies are buried in the cemetery. Why?"

Marley sat back in his chair and contemplated his coffee cup, swirling it in his hand and watching the whirlpool.

"Well," he continued, "that same evening I saw a wisp of a ghost in the sitting room. We haven't done much with that room except cleaning and electrical. I'm wondering who that ghost could have been."

Allie gave him a wink. "Oh, I bet you'll figure out a way to find out!"

*To find out, check out the second book in the Allie and Marley adventures. "The Mysterious Mansion Part 2" by Hank Roberts and/or "The Time Travelers" by Philip Levin*

Made in the USA
Monee, IL
14 July 2020